First U.S. edition 2007

Library of Congress Cataloging-in-Publication Data
is available.

Library of Congress Catalog Card Number pending

ISBN 978-0-7636-3404-9

Printed in China

2 4 6 8 10 9 7 5 3 1

This book was typeset in Windsor.
The illustrations were done in mixed media.

Candlewick Press
2067 Massachusetts Avenue
Cambridge, Massachusetts 02140

visit us at www.candlewick.com

Penguin

Polly Dunbar

CANDLEWICK PRESS
CAMBRIDGE, MASSACHUSETTS

Ben ripped open his present.

Inside was a penguin.

"Hello, Penguin!" said Ben.

"What shall we play?" said Ben.

Penguin said nothing.

"Can't you talk?" said Ben.

Penguin said nothing.

Ben tickled Penguin.

Penguin didn't laugh.

Ben made his funniest face
for Penguin.

Penguin didn't laugh.

Ben put on a happy hat

and sang a silly song

and did a dizzy dance.

Penguin said nothing.

"Will you talk to me if I stand on
my head?" said Ben.

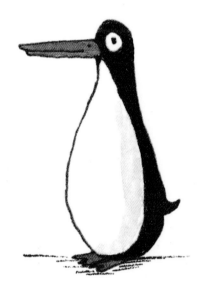

Penguin didn't say a word.

So Ben prodded Penguin

and stuck out his tongue at Penguin.

Penguin said nothing.

Ben made fun of Penguin

and imitated Penguin.

Penguin said nothing.

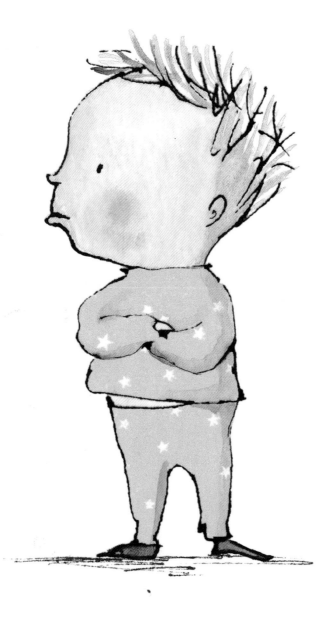

Ben ignored Penguin.

Penguin ignored Ben.

So Ben fired Penguin into outer space.

Penguin came back to Earth without a word.

Ben tried to feed Penguin
to a passing lion.

Penguin said nothing.

Lion didn't want to eat Penguin.

Ben got upset.

Penguin said nothing.

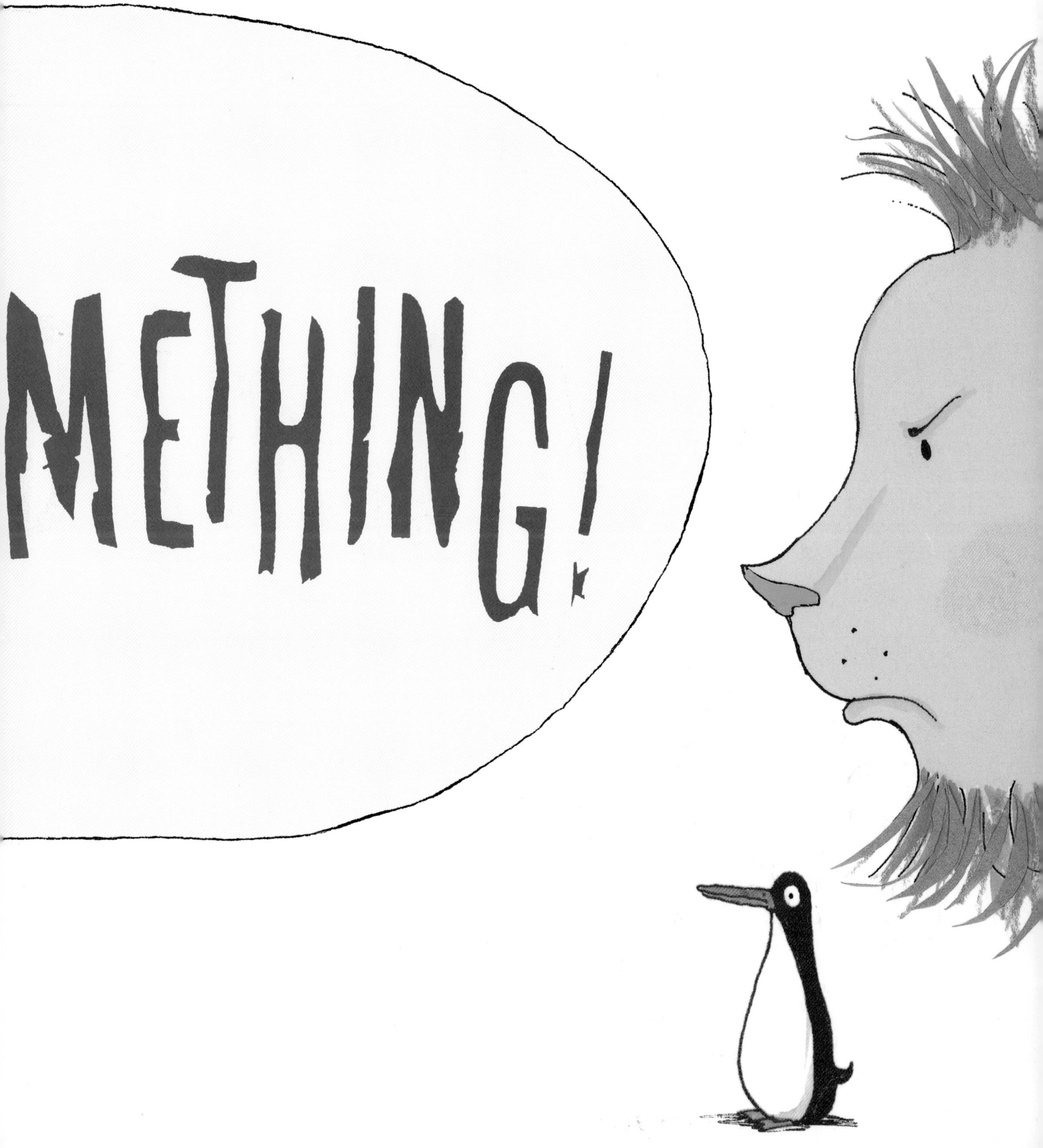
METHING!

Lion ate Ben

for being too noisy.

Penguin bit Lion
very hard
on the nose.

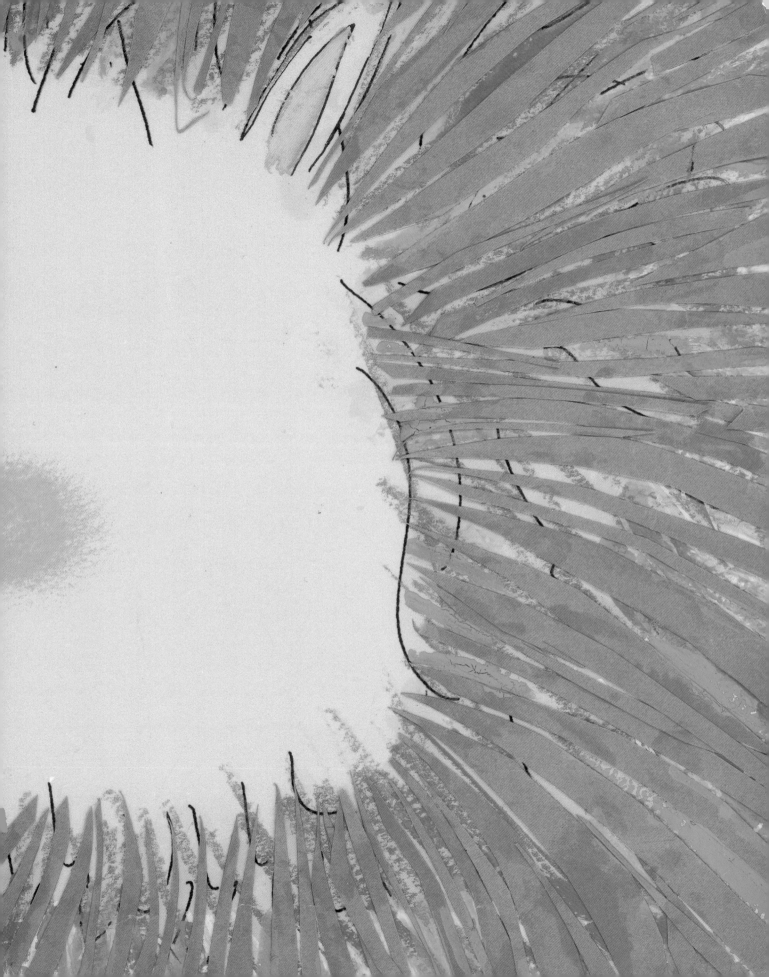

 said Lion.

 said Ben.

And Penguin said . . .

everything!